This book belongs to

....

IMAGINE THAT™

Licensed exclusively to Imagine That Publishing Ltd
Tide Mill Way, Woodbridge, Suffolk, IP12 1AP, UK
www.imaginethat.com
Copyright © 2021 Imagine That Group Ltd
All rights reserved
0 2 4 6 8 9 7 5 3 1
Manufactured in China

ISBN 978-1-80105-149-1

A catalogue record for this book is available from the British Library

5-minute
Mindful
Bedtime
Stories

Contents

Count My Blessings

Written by **Jeane Cabral**

Illustrated by **Gareth Llewhellin**

The Family Tree

Written by **Oakley Graham**

Illustrated by **P.S. Brooks**

Always There Bear

Written by **Trudi Granger**

Illustrated by **Gareth Llewhellin**

Bear's Little
Book of Calm

Written by
Seb Davey

Illustrated by
Julia Seal

Breathe. Count 1.

Calm.

Be still ...

It's good to take
things slow sometimes.

Breathe. Count 2.

Listen.

Really listen ...

What can
you hear?

Breathe. Count 3.

Look.

Notice things ...

What can you see?

Breathe. Count 4.

Feel.

Step outside ...

Feel the air on your skin.

Breathe. Count 5. **Hug.**

You're not alone ...

Enjoy the warmth of being together.

Breathe. Count 6.

Eat.

Take your time ...

Taste and appreciate every flavour.

Breathe. Count 7.

Talk.

Be open and honest ...

Share feelings
with yourself
and others.

Breathe. Count 8.

Share.

Share with your heart ...

Show your family that you
care about them.

Breathe. Count 9.

Focus.

Dream big ...

You can follow your dreams.

Breathe. Count 10.

Exercise.

Clear your thoughts ...

Enjoy and notice your surroundings.

Breathe.
Count 11.

Be quiet.

Listen to the sound
of your heart ...

Let everything else
drift away.

Breathe. Count 12.

Smile.

Be happy in the moment ...

Remember the good things about your day.

Calm.

Listen.

Look.

Feel.

Hug.

Eat.

Talk.

Share.

Focus.

Exercise.

Be quiet.

Smile.

Love Is ...

Written by
Noah James

Illustrated by
Gabi Murphy

Love is ...
A great big hug to say 'hello'.

Kisses when it's
time to go.

Chatting under
starry skies,

Looking up with
sleepy eyes.

Spending lots of time together,

In wind and rain – any weather!

Knowing what each other thinks,

Favourite foods, favourite drinks.

Dancing happy and carefree,

Like snowflakes
falling on the sea.

Building something fun together,

Memories that last forever.

Taking time to write a note,

Huddling underneath a coat.

Playing games all day long,

Making jokes, singing songs.

Open hearts and ears to listen,

When teary eyes are sad and glisten.

Someone who will always wait,

Even when you're
running late.

Love is ...

How I feel and act ...

... when I'm with you.

Star Light, Star Bright

Written by
Susie Linn

Illustrated by
Parwinder Singh

Star light, star bright,
The first star I see tonight,
I wish I may, I wish I might,
Have the wish I wish tonight.

Star light, star bright,
A wish I wish to make tonight.

I'd like my friend to come to stay,
And play with me for one whole day!

Star light, star bright,
A wish I wish to make tonight.

I'd love a bike to ride and race,
Around the park, from place to place.

Star light, star bright,
A wish I wish to make tonight.

A day with Mum and Dad, alone,
A great day out, or fun at home.

Star light, star bright,
A wish I wish to make tonight.

Big snowflakes fall while I'm asleep,
All bright and cold and very deep!

Star light, star bright,
A wish I wish to make tonight.

Make me strong so I can climb,
Up that big hill, time after time.

Star light, star bright,
A wish I wish to make tonight.
A superhero I will be,
Super-smart – hey, look at me!

Star light, star bright,
A wish I wish to make tonight.

I wish my birthday would come soon,
With party fun and big balloons!

Star light, star bright,
A wish I wish to make tonight.
A teddy bear, all fur and paws,
For play inside or play outdoors.

Star light, star bright,
A wish I wish to make tonight.

A windy day, my kite to fly,
And see it soaring, way up high!

Star light, star bright,
A wish I wish to make tonight.
A day full of my favourite treats,
My perfect things to do and eat!

Star light, star bright,
A wish I wish to make tonight.

That shooting stars will come my way,
To wish on every single day!

Count My Blessings

Written by
Jeane Cabral

Illustrated by
Gareth Llewhellin

I can count my blessings,
big and small.

Without them I would
have nothing at all.

I live in a home where
I'm safe and warm,

With family to love
me and keep me
from harm.

I have food to eat that keeps me strong.

It gives me energy all day long!

My teachers help me to learn and grow,

and teach me all that I need to know.

I have best friends for sharing and play.

They keep me so happy all through the day.

There are so many animals we can enjoy.

They help bring happiness to every girl and boy.

Plants and trees have special powers.

Trees give us shade and plants give us flowers.

I am so thankful we can breathe the air!

Although we can't see it, we still know it's there.

My mum and dad are a blessing to me.

They help me become the best I can be.

I may be the biggest
blessing there is!

I just open my heart and give!

The Family Tree

Written by
Oakley Graham

Illustrated by
P.S. Brooks

A small tree stood alone on a grassy hill.

The seasons changed and the tree
was sad and lonely as it grew.

The tree slept during the cold winters,
covered by a thick blanket of snow.

Then one day, after many years of growing,
something amazing happened ...

Chattering birds made nests in
the tree's strong branches.

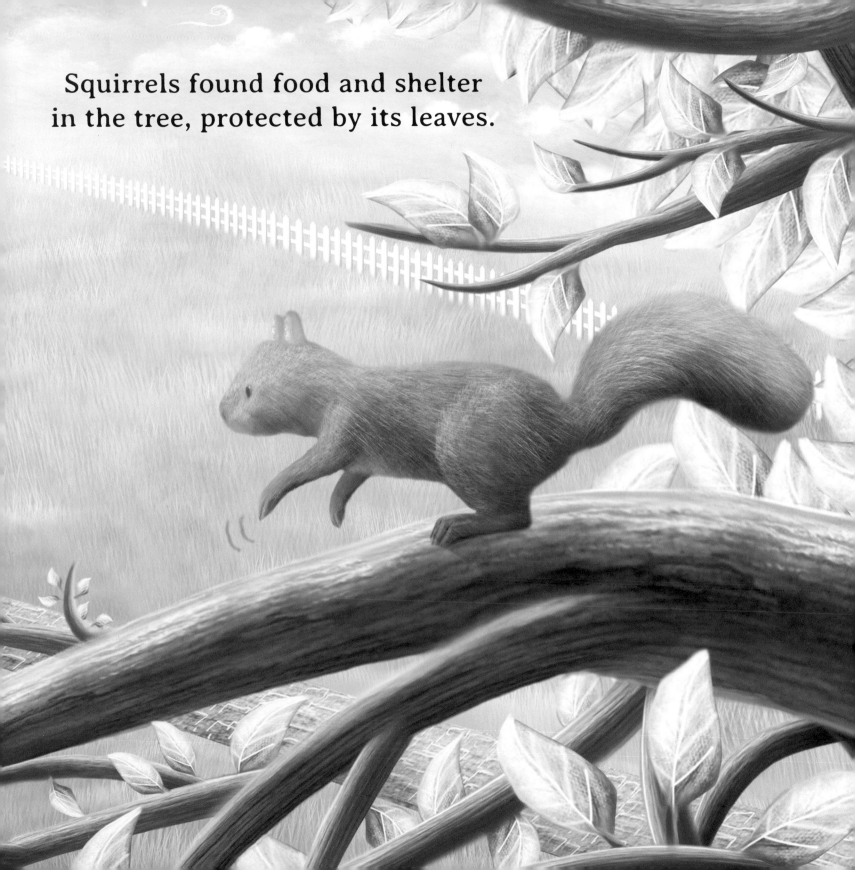

Squirrels found food and shelter in the tree, protected by its leaves.

On a fine spring day, a family came to live in a house
that was close to the tree.

The children played under the tree.

The children played around the tree.

The children even played and made
memories high up in the tree.

A big tree stood on a grassy hill,
but it was no longer alone ...

It was a family tree.

Always There Bear

Written by
Trudi Granger

Illustrated by
Gareth Llewhellin

Everyone needs a bear that's always there ...

A sunny, sandy seaside bear.

A much too wet to go outside bear.

A play-day with a friend at home bear.

A read a book alone bear.

A very happy birthday bear.

A sulky, grouchy, grumpy bear.

An in the car ... or bus
... or train bear.

A scoot ... or ride a trike ... or bike bear.

A full of bounce from toes to head bear.

A splashing, sploshing in a puddle bear.

A very quiet, need a cuddle bear.

A playing together in the park bear.

A stay close, keep safe after dark bear.

An icy, snowy, all gone white bear.

A bright and blowy, fly a kite bear.

Everyone needs a bear that's always there ...
An all day ... all night ... goodnight bear.